DAD JOKES

SO BAD, THEY'RE GOOD DAD JOKES

The
Terribly
Good
Dad jokes
Series
NO.1

FROM_ _ _ _ _ _ _ _ _ _

Printed Worldwide
First Printing, 2019

Dad, I'm sleepy!

a. Hi sleepy, I'm Dad!

Your brother left his bin on the floor.

His bin here?

Of course he's been here, he lives here!

**You know,
I can cut a piece of wood in half just by glancing at it.**

a. I saw it with my own two eyes!

You had the most stunning wedding!

a. Even the wedding cake was in tiers...

Did you hear about the French cheese factory that exploded?

A. It was covered in de Brie.

I dropped my instrument on my toe and broke it.

a. It was a heavy metal guitar.

Do you want to make this tissue dance?

a. Just put a little boogie in it!

Did you know skeletons are the most afraid Halloween creature?

a. They don't have any guts.

You know, Dad…

a. Of course I know Dad… I'm Dad!

Can I have a bookmark?

a. Sure, you can have a book, but my name is Dad, not Mark!

Don't look at the clock on daylight savings time.

a. It's rude to watch something while it changes.

I should get a Grammy for this present!

a. I'm such a good wrapper!

“Dad, why were you in the fireplace this morning?!”

a. “I wanted to sleep like a log!”

When your mom was pregnant with you, she wanted to go to a baby doctor.

a. But I wanted to go to a doctor that was a little older.

Why did you name your dance after the apocalypse?

a. I want to dance like there's no tomorrow!

My dentist has a crush on me!

a. She said she has fillings for me!

"I should turn left?"

"That's right!"

"So which is it? Left or right?"

I threw my clock out the window.

a. Watch out!

I'm trying to lose weight.

a. But I keep finding it again!

Did you know that French fries don't actually come from France?

a. They're actually made in Greece!

You know, that scarecrow won an award.

a. He was out standing in his field.

I'm serious, they gave me the wrong tool at the store!

a. This is not a drill!

“Someone told me you were turning into an owl.”

“Who?”

“I guess they were right.”

“Bye dad, I’m going on a trip!”

“Well I hope you land on something soft!”

You know, you could go to jail for not taking a nap.

a. They'd charge you with resisting a rest.

"Sorry I'm late, I was stuck in a traffic jam!"

a. "It's just a jar, why couldn't you go around it?"

Your school is taking you to a farm next week.

a. They said you're going on a field trip.

"Dad, I don't want to go to bed? I want to watch the cows a little longer!"

a. "Sorry, it's pasture bedtime!"

“Dad, I broke my arm in three places!”

a. “You probably shouldn’t go back to those places…”

Do you know why they only build chicken coops with two doors?

a. Because if they had four doors they’d be called chicken sedans.

"How is the book about zero gravity?"

a. "It's impossible to put down!"

The Indian restaurant makes so much money selling bread.

a. They're a naan-profit!

Did you hear the ghost was lonely?

a. Because he had no body.

Why are firefighters so fit?

a. Because they burn so many calories!

“Look at that fly, it doesn’t have any wings!”

a. “It’s actually called a walk.”

I ordered one egg and one chicken online!

a. I’ll let you know which comes first.

Hold on, there's something in my shoe.

a. Oh, never mind, it was my foot.

"Dad, how's your job at the coffee shop?"

a. "I'm getting a little tired of the daily grind."

My friend bet all his laundry when he was playing cards.

a. He put it all on the line.

"Dad, what language is spoken by the fewest people?"

a. "Sign language."

I once went to a farm where all the cows had no legs.

a. It's where we get ground beef!

A pumpkin pie costs $5 in Cuba, and a cherry pie costs $5.50 in Puerto Rico.

a. Those are the pie rates of the Caribbean.

Why are railroad conductors so good at their job?

a. Because they are so well trained.

I'm really slow with my condiments...

a. But I'll ketchup!

What is the most adorable angle?

a. Acute angle.

I got in a fight with a one-armed man.

a. He beat me single-handedly!

"How is your job crushing tin cans?"

a. "It's soda pressing."

I can't pick which shoe is the best.

a. They're tied!

“I’m cracking up!”

a. “Your skin looks smooth to me!”

“Dad, why aren’t you eating the sushi?”

a. “It looks a little fishy to me.”

I was wondering why the baseball seemed to be getting bigger.

a. And then it hit me!

"Dad, why is there a line outside that cemetery?"

a. "People are dying to get in!"

I saw a psychic who was really fat.

a. She was a four-chin teller.

Your mom keeps telling me she'll help me dig a hole and fill it with water.

a. I know she means well.

"I'm going to Sunday school, Dad."

a. "Have they taught you how to make a banana split yet?"

"Dad, today at school we learned about the rotation of the earth."

a. "Well that just makes my day!"

“Dad, I need to talk to you about your procrastinating.”

a. “Let’s talk about it later.”

You can’t eat cashews for every meal!

a. That’s just nuts.

Why is the Department of Justice so cold?

a. If it wasn't it would be called the Department of Just-water.

"Hey dad, do you want a Butterfinger?"

a. "Oh no, it slipped out of my hands!"

My math teacher used to love dessert.

a. He was always talking about pi.

I bought a broken kite…

a. …no strings attached.

I heard the restaurant they built in the International Space Station isn't very good.

a. It doesn't have much of an atmosphere.

You know, these noodles are fake…

a. They're impastas!

“Dad, do you think I look okay?”

a. “Let’s see. How many fingers am I holding up?”

“Dad, how many grapes grow on a vine?”

a. “I’m pretty sure all of them…”

“Dad, do you like being a plumber?”

a. “It’s sometimes hard watching your life’s work just go down the drain!”

Did you know that cavemen couldn’t hear pterodactyls going to the bathroom?

a. Because the pee is silent.

"Dad, why do you hate paper so much?"

a. "Because it's tearable..."

"I'm so happy, I'm going to water the flowers!"

a. "You're so excited you wet your plants!"

“What is your preferred number system?”

a. “I, for one, use Roman numerals.”

Someone stole my coffee!

a. I got mugged!

"Where did you get that prosthetic arm?"

a. "At the second hand store."

"Dad, do you like your facial hair?"

a. "Yes, but I mustache your opinion!"

"Dad, there's nothing written on the rules you gave me."

a. "Yeah, they're unwritten rules."

"Dad, why did you become a photographer?"

a. "I liked taking photos, so I figured I'd take a shot."

I don't believe atoms.

a. They make up everything!

There was a kidnapping just next door.

a. He woke up though.

Mom just told me her face is fake.

a. She said it's made up!

I sing solo sometimes!

a. Solo that no one can hear me.

"You know, I'm named after George Washington."

"But your name is Dave..."

"I know. I was named after George Washington, a couple hundred years."

"Dad, why are you doing somersaults all over the place?"

a. "It's just how I roll!"

“Dad, did you get a haircut?”

a. “No, I got all of them cut.”

“Dad, can you make me pancakes.”

“Sure!”

“Dad! Why are you trying to put me on the stove?!”

“You said you wanted me to make you pancakes…”

In 2021, we'll probably know exactly what we should have done the year before.

a. Hindsight is 2020!

My coworker just quit his job because the mirrors were too cloudy.

a. He couldn't see himself working there.

"How did you figure out how to work the seatbelt?"

a. "It just clicked!"

"Why did you hit me after you told the joke?"

a. "Because it was the punchline!"

Do you know why elephants are such good swimmer?

a. Because they have trunks!

“I’m so sorry about the wait!”

a. “Are you calling me fat?”

Did you hear the guy who invented the throat lozenge got cremated?

a. There wasn't a coffin at his funeral.

"I wish I was rich!"

a. "You could always just change your name!"

"Do you want the soda in a bag?"

a. "No, please leave it in the bottle."

The Pope has the bird flu.

a. One of his Cardinals gave it to him!

Did you hear they let babies join the army?

a. They formed an infantry!

If Lassie could see these dogs today...

a. She'd be rolling over in her grave!

"The answer to this math problem is zero."

a. "Wow, thanks for nothing!"

I'll use a stencil or a compass...

a. ... but using a ruler is where I draw the line!

If I had a quarter for every time someone told me I was bad at math...

a. I'd have $9.99.

Dad, do you like my sneakers?

a. Yes! Do they help you walk around quietly?

Made in the USA
Middletown, DE
16 June 2022

67247576R00031